New Girl

Bimi

Twink

Pix

Sooze

Sili

Zena

Mariella

Lola

Glitterwings Academy

Book Seven

New Girl

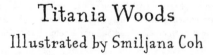

Titania Woods

Illustrated by Smiljana Coh

BLOOMSBURY
CHILDREN'S
BOOKS

First published in Great Britain in 2008 by Bloomsbury Publishing Plc
36 Soho Square, London, W1D 3QY

Text copyright © Lee Weatherly 2008
Illustrations copyright © Smiljana Coh 2008
The moral rights of the author and illustrator have been asserted

ISBN 978 0 7475 9204 4

All papers used by Bloomsbury Publishing are natural, recyclable products made
from wood grown in well-managed forests. The manufacturing processes conform to
the environmental regulations of the country of origin.

Typeset by Dorchester Typesetting Group Ltd
Printed in Singapore by Tien Wah Press

1 3 5 7 9 10 8 6 4 2

www.glitterwingsacademy.co.uk

To Julie, who gave the fairies their fashion show

Chapter One

'Oh, how beautiful!' breathed Twink Flutterby.

She tipped her head back to take in the glittering crystal cavern around her. The underground room sparkled with pinks and greens and blues. It was like being inside a diamond!

'Isn't it glimmery?' said Bimi Bluebell, her best friend. 'The Crystal Caverns are my favourite place in the world. It's so great to show them to you!'

'I love them!' Twink flew to Bimi's side and squeezed her hand. 'This is the best holiday ever, Bimi.'

The two fairies smiled warmly at each other. Both were second-year students at Glitterwings Academy, and had been best friends since their very first term. Now Twink was staying with Bimi's family over the holidays, and Bimi's dad had taken them to see the famous caverns.

'Shall we move on to the next cavern, girls?' he asked now, flying over to them from where he had been examining a cluster of crystals.

'Ooh, yes!' cried Bimi, giving a little skip. 'It's my favourite. Twink, just wait till you see it!'

Twink nodded, smiling shyly. She still felt just a little bit bashful around Mr Bluebell – he was the most handsome fairy she had ever seen. No wonder Bimi was so pretty, she thought, with a mother and father who both looked like they should be in petal mags!

The passageway between the caverns shimmered like a rainbow trapped in ice. Twink flitted down it with Bimi and her dad, gazing about her in awe.

'What's in there?' Twink asked suddenly. They were passing the entrance to a small chamber.

Peering inside, she could just make out a single large crystal, standing by itself on a stone pillar.

'Nothing for us,' said Bimi's father with a laugh, shepherding her onwards. 'It's a crystal that will show you your fortune, if you ask it.'

'*Really?*' gasped Twink, forgetting her shyness. 'But that's amazing!' She looked over her shoulder at the disappearing doorway.

'I think it sounds creepy,' said Bimi with a shudder. 'What if it showed you something awful?'

Her dad grinned. 'Well, they say it will show you exactly what will happen – if you look into it, that is. Best to stay away from that sort of magic, and just enjoy the crystals for their beauty. Look, Twink – the Grand Chamber!'

He motioned with a flourish as they entered the largest, most spectacular cave of all. Green and blue crystals sparkled down its walls like frozen water-falls. A massive crystal sat in the centre of the tall chamber, reflecting the shimmering rainbow light around the room.

Twink exclaimed in delight . . . but part of her

was still thinking about the little room off the passageway. Could that crystal *really* tell you your fortune? What would it show her, if she asked it?

High up on the other side of the cavern, a guide was giving a flighted tour to a group of fairies.

'Shall we join them?' suggested Bimi's dad. The three of them took off, hovering on the edge of the group.

'This room is also known as the Singing Chamber,' the guide was saying, bobbing in the air before them. 'The crystals sing songs to each other, you see. If you all close your eyes and concentrate, you should be able to hear them.'

'This bit is really glimmery,' whispered Bimi in Twink's ear. 'You have to concentrate hard, though – it takes a while to hear anything.'

Twink shut her eyes along with the others . . . but after a moment she took a peek. Everyone was hovering with their eyes closed, straining to hear. Even the guide had his eyes shut.

Twink's heart pounded. Did she dare? No, she couldn't, she shouldn't . . . oh, but a crystal that could tell her fortune! How could she resist *that*?

Before she could talk herself out of it, Twink plunged into a steep dive, slicing through the cavern like an arrow. In a flash, she had swooped through the doorway and was skimming down the passage, the wind whistling through her pink hair.

She landed at the entrance to the little chamber. Inside, the crystal gleamed on its stone stand. Twink hesitated. Did she really dare? But there was no time to lose; Bimi and her dad might see that she was missing at any moment! Twink flew into the room.

The crystal was an irregular shape, like an iceberg that sat balanced on its point. Twink edged up to it. She could see herself reflected in its many facets, her eyes wide and frightened.

Her voice came out in a strangled squeak. 'Um – would you show me my fortune, please?'

She stared anxiously into the crystal. Its facets gleamed coolly back at her. The seconds ticked past.

Finally Twink smiled and let out a breath. There had been nothing to it after all; Bimi's father had only been joking. What an idiot she had been to fall for it!

She turned away to fly back to the others – and then stopped short. A swirling mist had appeared in the crystal's depths. Twink leaned forward, her heart beating wildly. The mist cleared, and an image came into view.

'Oh!' she cried. It was Glitterwings Academy!

The familiar oak tree sat on its grassy hill, its leaves ablaze with orange and yellow. Twink stared open-mouthed. There was no sound, but she could

see crowds of young fairies hovering about the tree, smiling and chatting to each other. It was so real!

As she watched, two more fairies flew up the hill: one with pink hair and one with blue. Twink gasped as she realised it was herself and Bimi. Then Bimi's father came into view, carrying their oak-leaf bags. Why, she was looking at tomorrow, the first day of the new autumn term!

An uncertain frown touched her face. But . . . why did she seem so unhappy?

The Twink in the crystal was flying slowly, with her head down. And Bimi's usual smile was gone. Instead, Twink's best friend had an exasperated grimace on her face. The two fairies flew side by side, not speaking to each other.

Twink's wings felt clammy as she gazed into the crystal. What was going on? Were she and Bimi going to have a quarrel?

The scene changed. Suddenly Twink saw Bimi talking and laughing with a fairy she didn't recognise: a very pretty fairy with curly lilac hair and purple wings. The Twink in the crystal hovered nearby, looking left-out and miserable. As Twink watched, Bimi linked arms with the strange fairy and flew away with her, leaving the Twink in the crystal staring sadly after them.

Twink watched numbly, unable to believe what she was seeing.

Other scenes flashed into view, faster and faster. Bimi and the new girl were flying to class together, hovering side by side in the library, sitting next to each other in lessons. The new fairy even had Twink's usual bed beside Bimi in Peony Branch! And in every image, Twink saw herself on the side-lines, dejected and alone.

'Oh,' whispered Twink as the crystal finally went dark. The cavern felt icy-cold. 'Bimi will have a new best friend! She'll forget all about me . . .'

Then she shook herself. It *couldn't* be true! Bimi was the best friend in the world. 'I don't believe you,' she burst out to the crystal, clenching her fists. 'Bimi would *never* do that!'

The crystal sat silently on its pedestal, winking in the dim light.

Suddenly desperate to get away, Twink skimmed quickly from the room. Her thoughts tumbled like autumn leaves as she raced back to the Grand Chamber. *Of course* Bimi would never abandon her! Yet the images had looked so real . . . and hadn't Bimi's father said that the crystal would show you exactly what would happen?

It must be true, then, thought Twink, fighting tears as she flew into the cavern. *Oh, I wish I had never looked into it!* Mr Bluebell had been right to steer them past the crystal. Why hadn't she listened to him?

It felt like she had been gone for ages, but the group of hovering fairies were only just opening their eyes when Twink jetted up next to them. She tried to look relaxed, as if she had been there all along.

'A lovely song from the crystals, as always!' The guide looked as pleased as if he had sung it himself. 'And now, if you'll just follow me, I'll show you a most unusual formation . . .' The group began moving off.

'Wasn't that glimmery?' said Bimi. Her smile faded when she saw Twink's expression. 'What's wrong? Didn't you hear the song?'

Twink shrugged. 'Sort of. It was OK, I suppose.' She knew that if she tried to say anything else, she'd burst into tears.

Bimi's blue eyebrows rose in surprise. 'Oh! I thought you'd really like it.'

'I did! I said it was OK, didn't I?' Twink's throat felt like she had swallowed an acorn.

'Well, maybe crystal songs aren't everyone's cup of dew,' laughed Bimi's father. He put a hand on each of their shoulders, steering them from the cavern. 'Come on, girls – let's go and get a bite of seed cake in the Crystal Cafe.'

Bimi's family lived in a spreading butterfly bush, with sweet-smelling purple flowers dangling all about. It was nearing dusk as they returned, and Twink could see the small round windows at the bush's base glowing with a welcome golden light.

'Is everything all right?' whispered Bimi as they

flew through the front door. 'You seem really down.'

Twink managed a smile. 'Yes, of course! Sorry . . . I'm just tired.'

'I'm worn out, too,' said Bimi's dad with a yawn. 'You girls are exhausting! I'll be glad when you go back to school tomorrow, and I can have some peace and quiet.'

Twink knew he was only teasing, but at the mention of school her spirits dropped still further. She swallowed hard, dreading what might happen the next day.

When they ate dinner that night, Twink played with her food. She could feel Bimi watching her in growing bewilderment, but she couldn't help it. Over and over, she kept seeing the images of Bimi and the new girl in her mind, until she had no appetite at all.

'Would you like some nectar, Twink?' asked Mrs Bluebell, offering the pecan-shell pitcher. She was just as pretty as her daughter, with the same dark blue hair and unusual silver and gold wings, and always looked extremely stylish.

'Oh! Um . . . no, thank you,' stammered Twink, jolted from her thoughts. 'Sorry, I was just . . . thinking of school tomorrow.' She felt the tips of her pointed ears grow warm as Bimi gave her a searching look.

The Bluebell family's dining room was in the centre of the bush's trunk, and was perfectly circular, with a polished black stone table and elegant walnut-shell chairs. A large petal tapestry hung on the wall.

It was far grander than any room in Twink's own home, and suddenly she felt a pang for her family's friendly, chaotic tree stump beside its woodland stream. She'd give anything to be back there now, and for none of this to have ever happened!

'Speaking of school, I got a petal today from Mirabel,' said Mrs Bluebell, placing the pitcher back on to the table. 'Bimi, do you remember her from that party I gave last year?'

Bimi's face lit up. 'Mirabel Moonglow? Of course!' She turned eagerly to Twink. 'She's one of Mum's old friends from modelling. Now she's a fashion designer, and really famous. She's in the petal mags all the time!'

'I think I've heard of her,' said Twink, interested despite herself. 'Were you really a model, Mrs Bluebell?'

Mrs Bluebell smiled. 'Yes, didn't Bimi ever tell you? Mirabel's a good friend of mine from those days. She always had a flair for design. This is one of hers, in fact!' She motioned to her shimmering cobweb dress.

'It looks lovely on you,' said Mr Bluebell admiringly. 'You could still model now, if you wanted to – you're just as beautiful as the day I first met you!'

Twink saw Bimi grimace, and winced in sympathy. It was awful when parents started getting lovey-dovey in front of your friends.

'Anyway, Mirabel says that her daughter Kiki is going to be starting school at Glitterwings tomorrow,' continued Mrs Bluebell. 'She wasn't getting on very well at Emerald Leaf – she found the girls there much too snobbish.'

Bimi shuddered. 'Oh, I've heard those Emerald Leaf fairies are awful! I don't blame her a bit, do you, Twink?'

'Er . . . no,' said Twink. Suddenly her heart was pounding. *A new girl! I bet she's the one,* she thought wildly.

'Kiki's a second-year student as well,' went on Mrs Bluebell. 'Would you look out for her, Bimi, and make her feel at home?'

'Of course!' said Bimi. 'It must be terrible starting a new school mid-year. We'll both be really nice to

21

her, won't we, Twink?'

Twink felt as if her wings had turned to stone. Everyone was looking at her, waiting for her response. 'Yes, of course,' she mumbled.

She saw Bimi's expression turn puzzled, and looked quickly down at her clover-leaf plate. Later that evening, when she and Bimi were packing their things for the next day, Twink cleared her throat.

'What's Kiki like?' she asked casually. They were in Bimi's bedroom, a small, pretty branch filled with tiny dewdrop ornaments and delicate petal pillows.

Bimi looked up from packing her oak-leaf bag. 'I don't know; I've never met her. Her mother's really nice, though.'

'Well . . . what does she look like?' Twink put a stack of crisp new petal pads into her bag, thinking of the pretty lilac-haired fairy from the crystal.

Bimi's eyebrows drew together. 'You mean Kiki? How should I know?'

Twink shrugged. 'I just thought you might have seen a drawing of her sometime, or that maybe your mum told you what she looks like . . .' she trailed off, realising how ridiculous she sounded.

Bimi propped her hands on her hips. 'Why would we talk about Kiki's looks? Twink, what's *up* with you? You've been acting weird since this afternoon!'

Twink forced a laugh. 'Nothing! It's just that her mum used to be a model, so . . . so I wondered if she was as pretty as her mum, that's all. Like you and *your* mum.'

Bimi scowled in embarrassment. She was very shy about her beauty, and never liked talking about it. 'I don't know,' she said crossly, shoving a pair of grass socks into her bag. 'You can see for yourself tomorrow!'

'Sorry,' muttered Twink.

Bimi took a deep breath. 'That's OK. But Twink, it's stupid comparing me to my mum. I could never be like her, no matter what.'

'What do you mean?' asked Twink. 'You look just like her!'

Bimi made a face as she tucked a pair of pixie boots in alongside the socks. 'Not *that*.

Just . . . I could never be brave enough to model, that's all.'

Twink stared at her. 'Do you *want* to model?'

A bright flush raced up Bimi's cheeks. 'No, of course not!' she said quickly. 'Don't talk about it, OK?'

'OK,' echoed Twink in confusion. *Bimi*, wanting to model? It was true that Bimi was much more interested in fashion than Twink, but she was so shy! The thought that she might want to model had never even occurred to Twink.

Feeling somehow worse than before, Twink returned to her packing. A pause lengthened and grew between the two girls.

'Twink, what's wrong?' asked Bimi softly. 'Please tell me – I can tell *something* is.'

The words stuck in Twink's throat. She couldn't tell Bimi the awful things she had seen, she just couldn't!

'I suppose I'm not ready to go back to school yet, that's all,' she said finally, fiddling with the bark clasp on her bag. 'It's been such a glimmery holiday.'

Bimi looked uncertain. 'Twink, are you *sure* that's all it is?'

'I'm sure,' said Twink shortly, turning away.

Her spirits felt leaden as they finished packing. Bimi's room was so small that she was sleeping in a silken hammock near the ceiling, and when it was time for bed she flew up to it glumly.

'Well, goodnight,' said Bimi, sounding bewildered.

'Goodnight,' Twink mumbled back.

Bimi turned the glow-worm lantern off, and the little room plunged into shadows. Twink lay huddled in her hammock, staring into the darkness long after Bimi had fallen asleep.

For the first time in her life, she wasn't looking forward to going to Glitterwings.

Chapter Two

The journey from Bimi's house to Glitterwings Academy took them over sunlit meadows, rich with autumn beauty. Twink hardly noticed. She followed along after Bimi and her father, glumly aware that every wing stroke took her closer and closer to the fortune foretold by the crystal.

'What have you girls got packed in here, anyway?' grumbled Bimi's dad good-naturedly. He was carrying both of their oak-leaf bags for them.

'Rocks, of course!' teased Bimi.

Her smile faded as she glanced back at Twink. She

let out an exasperated huff, clearly tired of her friend's mood. Twink quickly put on a smile, but Bimi had already skimmed away, talking pointedly with her dad.

Twink bit her lip and put on a burst of speed to catch up with them. The three fairies crested a hill, and then suddenly, there it was – Glitterwings Academy.

The massive oak tree looked exactly as it had in the crystal, its leaves ablaze with reds and yellows. Hundreds of tiny golden windows twisted gracefully up the oak tree's trunk, and the grand double doors at its base stood open in welcome.

Just as Twink had seen the day before, groups of brightly dressed fairies hovered about the tree, swapping stories of their summer holidays. Twink's stomach felt cold as they drew closer. Was there a fairy with curly lilac hair among them?

'Here at last!' grinned Bimi's father as they landed. He dropped their bags with mock relief. 'Now, you girls have a good term. Twink, be sure to write to your parents and let them know you got here safely.'

'I will,' said Twink shyly. 'And thank you and Mrs Bluebell for having me to stay with you – I had a wonderful time.'

'We enjoyed having you,' smiled Bimi's father. 'Bimi's always spent too much time on her own; it's good for her to have a friend to stay.'

Would she and Bimi still *be* friends after this term? Twink swallowed hard, wondering if she could somehow ask Mr Bluebell about crystal fortunes. Did they always have to come true?

'What is it, Twink?' Bimi's dad raised a friendly eyebrow.

'Er – nothing,' said Twink hastily, colouring up. 'Thanks again, that's all!'

'Bye, Dad,' said Bimi, clasping him affectionately around the neck. 'See you at the end of term!' A few moments later Mr Bluebell was skimming away over the hill, waving over his shoulder.

Bimi gave Twink a quizzical look. 'What were you going to say to my dad?'

'Nothing!' said Twink, smiling widely. 'Um, I suppose we'd better get checked in. Where's

Miss Sparkle?'

Bimi started to say something else, and then stopped with a sigh. 'There she is,' she said, pointing to their year head – a serious-looking fairy with gauzy white wings you could almost see through. 'Come on.'

Picking up their bags, they flitted across to where Miss Sparkle stood on one of the tree roots. She ticked them off her clover-leaf pad without a smile.

'Miss Sparkle, do you know if Kiki Moonglow has arrived yet?' Bimi's pretty cheeks reddened slightly. 'She's a new second-year student . . . our mums are friends, and my mum told me to watch out for her.'

'I see.' Miss Sparkle still didn't smile, but her dour expression lightened slightly. She consulted her clover pad. 'Yes, she's here. She's going to be in Peony Branch as well.'

'Oh, she's in our branch! How funny!' burst out Bimi.

Twink couldn't say anything. It felt as if she had turned to stone.

'She's just over there saying goodbye to her

mother, if you want to go over,' continued Miss Sparkle. 'I'm sure she'll be glad to see some friendly faces.'

Dreading what she might see, Twink looked over to where Miss Sparkle had pointed with her wing. A fairy with long, curly lilac hair and purple wings stood on the lawn nearby, talking to an older fairy who was clearly her mum.

A chill swept over Twink. It was her! The fairy from the crystal.

'Ooh, yes, that's Mirabel Moonglow!' said Bimi. 'Come on, Twink, let's go and say hello.'

Feeling like she was in a nightmare, Twink flitted slowly along behind Bimi. Her friend was too excited to notice the expression on her face – which was just as well, since Twink knew that her smile must look more like a sickly grimace.

'Hello, Mrs Moonglow!' said Bimi as she landed. 'Do you remember me? I'm –'

'Bimi!' exclaimed the woman. 'Of course I know you; you look just like your mum.'

It was easy to see that Mrs Moonglow used to be a

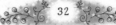

model, thought Twink, hovering uncertainly to one side. She was very tall, with wavy purple hair and shimmering violet wings. Her leafy green dress swirled gracefully about her.

'Bimi, this is Kiki, my daughter,' went on Mrs Moonglow, putting her hand on the curly-haired fairy's shoulder.

'Hi!' said Kiki. Close up, Twink could see that the new girl had a sprinkling of freckles across her nose. She wore a stylish rose-petal dress, and had a bright, friendly smile.

'Hi, Kiki – welcome to Glitterwings!' said Bimi, touching wings with her. 'I'm sure you'll like it much better here than at Emerald Leaf. I've heard that the fairies there are *horrible*.'

'Don't remind me!' laughed Kiki. 'But Mum said *your* mum is always saying how much you love it here at Glitterwings, so I thought I'd give it a try.'

'Oh, it's the best school in the world!' said Bimi earnestly. 'Isn't it, Twink? Oh, sorry – this is my friend Twink Flutterby,' she added to Kiki and her mum. 'We're all going to be in Peony Branch together!'

'Hi,' said Twink. Her smile felt like it might crumble away into dust. 'Yeah, it's . . . it's really glimmery. You'll love it here.'

'Well, I can see that you girls have it all under control,' laughed Mrs Moonglow. 'Goodbye, Kiki – have a good term!'

After Mrs Moonglow had flown away, Bimi turned to Kiki. 'Come on, we'll show you where our branch is, and then we can give you a quick tour of the school!'

'Glimmery!' Kiki picked up a bulging oak-leaf bag. 'I'm so glad you go to this school too, Bimi. It's great to have someone to show me around.'

'I'm happy to do it!' said Bimi. 'You can ask us anything you want – can't she, Twink?' Bimi's bright smile faded as she glanced at Twink, who stood to one side, biting her lip.

Twink quickly tried to rearrange her expression into something more welcoming. 'Of course she can!'

'Come on, Kiki,' said Bimi, giving Twink an odd look.

The three fairies flew towards the open double doors at the tree's base, dodging through a crowd of older fairies. Twink was silent as Bimi and Kiki chattered away. She had a sudden memory of the first day of the last term, when she and Bimi had flown into school together arm in arm.

Now Bimi was hardly even looking at her. 'Here's the inside!' she said, hovering. 'What do you think, Kiki?'

The inside of Glitterwings was like a high, high

tower filled with soft golden light. Branches shot off in all directions, as far up as the eye could see. Fairies flitted in and out of them like darting birds, shouting and calling to each other.

'Oh!' Kiki flew in a slow circle, staring upwards. 'Isn't it beautiful? It just goes on for ever!'

Twink looked away. It seemed doubly cruel that not only was Bimi going to go off with Kiki, but Twink had to pretend to like her as well. *I should just leave them to it,* she thought miserably. *What do they need* me *for?*

'Peony Branch is almost at the very top,' said

Bimi. 'Come on!'

As they spiralled up the trunk, Bimi pointed out branches to Kiki. 'That's our Creature Kindness branch. Mr Woodleaf is so funny; he's practically terrified of us! And that's where we have Fairy Dust lessons. Miss Sparkle seems really grim at first, but she's OK really . . .'

Finally they came to a branch with a large pink peony hanging upside-down over its ledge. Bimi landed with a flourish. 'And this is our branch!'

'Glimmery!' Kiki peered over the side. 'Look how far up we are!'

Twink suddenly remembered something else the crystal had shown her . . . Kiki was going to have her old bed, beside Bimi. *I suppose I'll be off to the side with Mariella,* she thought sullenly, thinking of an unpleasant fairy in their branch.

'Could I ask you both a favour before we go inside?' asked Kiki, straightening up again.

'Of course!' said Bimi.

'Sure,' mumbled Twink. *Maybe she's going to ask if she can have my cupboard, too,* she thought.

'It's just . . . would you mind not saying who my mum is? Don't get me wrong, I'm really proud of her,' said Kiki quickly. 'But sometimes fairies act strangely when they find out I'm her daughter – like wanting to be my best friend when they hardly even know me.'

Bimi gave a sympathetic shudder. 'Don't worry, we won't say anything – will we, Twink?'

'No,' said Twink dully. She couldn't feel very sorry for Kiki, somehow.

'Great!' said Kiki in obvious relief. 'I'd rather that everyone just liked me for myself. If they're going to like me at all, that is!' she added with a grin.

Bimi pushed open the door, and the three fairies flew inside. Peony Branch was a long, curving branch filled with sunlight. A large pink peony hung over each mossy bed like a canopy, and cunning little bark cupboards were tucked away here and there.

Several of the other girls had already arrived, and were chatting to each other as they unpacked. 'Hello, Opposite!' called a fairy with lavender hair and dancing violet eyes. 'Who have you got there?'

'Hi, Sooze,' said Twink with a weak smile. Sooze always called her 'Opposite', because Twink had pink hair and lavender wings – the exact *opposite* to Sooze. 'This is Kiki . . . she's new.'

'Hi,' said Kiki, putting down her bag. 'What a great branch!'

'Well, *we* like it,' laughed Sooze. She came flitting over with a few of the others to say hello. Twink could tell straight away that they approved of the new girl, which just made things worse, somehow.

'Where would you like to sleep, Kiki?' said Bimi eagerly.

Twink saw that her and Bimi's old beds from last term were still vacant, and she held her breath. *Oh, please,* she thought. *Let the crystal be wrong. Let Bimi want to have the bed next to me, same as always!*

'Well, why don't we all three sleep in a row?' suggested Kiki, including Twink in her smile. 'See, there are three beds together here – perfect!'

'Great!' Bimi flitted to the middle bed and put her things down. Kiki placed her own bag on Twink's old bed, and the two girls began to unpack.

Twink flew slowly to the bed that was left. At least she was beside Bimi . . . but somehow it wasn't at all as she had imagined. Bimi hadn't even looked at her to see whether she was happy with the arrangement.

'Where did you go to school before, Kiki?' called Mariella from across the branch.

Mariella, a pointy-faced fairy with long, silvery-green hair, had been thoroughly horrid for most of the time Twink had known her . . . until the previous term, when she had finally been forced to face up to her unpleasant behaviour. Now she was something of a reformed character, though Twink sometimes thought she was just as unpleasant as before, only in a different way!

Kiki made a face. 'Emerald Leaf.'

Mariella's jaw dropped. '*Really?*' she gasped. 'I'd give anything to go there!'

'Rather you than me,' said Kiki, arranging a drawing of her family on her bedside mushroom. 'The girls there were all stuck-up little beetles!'

The branch burst out laughing at the expression

on Mariella's face.

'You don't know it, Kiki, but you're talking to the *original* stuck-up little beetle,' said Sooze with a wicked grin.

'Oh, shut up,' snapped Mariella, tossing her hair. 'But Kiki, your family must be awfully important for you to go to Emerald Leaf.'

Kiki shrugged. Twink saw the tips of her pointed ears turn red. 'Not especially.'

Without warning, Mariella skimmed across the branch and picked up the drawing of Kiki's family.

'Are these your parents?' she asked innocently. 'Your mum's really pretty.'

Kiki started to say something and stopped, colouring up.

'Mariella, put it down!' burst out Bimi. 'It's none of your business.'

'Watch it, Mosquito Nose,' said Sooze warningly, narrowing her eyes at Mariella.

'Hang on, I think I recognise her,' said Mariella, squinting at the drawing. 'She's not wearing that glittery make-up she wears in the petal mags, but . . . oh, I know!' she squealed suddenly. 'It's *Mirabel Moonglow,* the fashion designer!'

Chapter
Three

Kiki grabbed the drawing back. 'Yes, all right,' she said crossly. 'But don't go *on* about it, will you?'

Mariella's eyes were like shining stars. '*And* she used to be a famous model!' she breathed. 'Oh, you're so lucky! You must know so many famous fairies! You –'

Kiki let out a heavy sigh. 'You see what I mean?' she said to Bimi.

'Kiki doesn't want to be treated any differently because of who her mum is,' Bimi told the branch. 'She just wants to be herself.'

Pix, a clever fairy with short red hair, nodded approvingly. 'I don't blame you, Kiki. Don't worry, you won't get any special treatment from us!'

'That means *you*, Mosquito Nose!' put in Sooze, flitting across and dragging Mariella back to her own bed.

'What?' protested Mariella as Sooze sat her down firmly. 'I didn't do anything!'

Twink had kept quiet through all of this, woodenly unpacking her things. Placing a drawing of her own family on her bedside mushroom, she stared down at their smiling faces with a homesick pang. She could tell already what a miserable term this was going to be.

With a rustle and a thump, Mrs Hover the matron arrived. 'Whoo!' she huffed, patting her light pink hair into place. 'I certainly get my exercise, flying all the way up here! Has everyone arrived?'

She counted them quickly, and nodded. 'Excellent! Now come along, everyone, it's time for the opening session in the Great Branch.'

As the fairies flitted towards the door, Bimi took Twink's arm, holding her back. 'What's wrong?' she whispered. 'You've hardly said two words to Kiki!'

Twink lifted a wing. 'I don't know. I'm just sort of . . . tired, that's all.'

Bimi looked cross. 'Like you were tired this morning, and last night? Twink, what's *up* with you? Why can't you tell me what's wrong?'

'*Nothing's* wrong, I keep telling you!' insisted Twink, pulling away. Bimi had read her mind so many times before – surely she'd know how sad and frightened Twink felt now, at the prospect of losing her best friend?

But Bimi just shook her head. 'Fine, have it your way,' she said wearily.

Skimming quickly away, Bimi caught up with Kiki at the door. The two fairies flew out of the branch together without a backward look.

The Great Branch was the largest branch in the school, with high, arching windows and rows of mossy tables. A different flower hung over each table for each of the branches, making the long room look like a garden wonderland.

When Twink arrived at the Peony Branch table, she saw Bimi and Kiki already sitting side by side. Her cheeks on fire, Twink hastily sat down on the first empty mushroom she saw, beside a tall fairy called Zena.

'Hi, Zena, how were your hols?' she asked brightly.

'Great!' said Zena, tucking back a strand of yellow hair. 'We visited my cousin at Shining Lake, and I learned how to surf on the back of a fish – it was glimmery! How about you?'

At the other end of the table, Bimi and Kiki were chatting away as if they had known each other for years. Sooze and Pix leaned towards them, joining in. As Twink watched, Kiki laughed at something Bimi had said, fluttering her purple wings.

A sour taste twisted at the back of Twink's throat. And Kiki had said she didn't like a fuss made over her! Well, she looked as if she were enjoying it, thought Twink. And making them promise not to say who her mum was – why, she had probably been *thrilled* when Mariella worked it out!

'Twink?' Zena raised her eyebrows questioningly.

Twink started. 'Oh! Sorry – what did you say?'

Before Zena could reply, Miss Shimmery, the HeadFairy, took to the air at the front of the Branch and clapped her hands for attention. The Great Branch fell silent as the students all turned to face her.

'Welcome to a new term at Glitterwings,' she announced in her low, rich voice. Her rainbow wings caught the light as she hovered. 'And a very special welcome to all our new girls – we hope you'll be very happy here.'

She smiled warmly at the Peony Branch table. Kiki smiled back, and Twink made a face before she could help herself.

Noticing Zena looking strangely at her, Twink stared down at the table as Miss Shimmery made the usual announcements: no high-speed flying in the school, uniforms required from tomorrow, complete with oak-leaf cap . . .

The HeadFairy gazed meaningfully at the older years, who left their caps off at every opportunity. Good-natured groans filled the Branch.

'And finally, I've some exciting news,' said Miss Shimmery. 'Though we had our annual school exhibition early last year, our older girls will know that it normally takes place now, in the autumn term.'

The exhibition! Twink looked up as a prickle of interest raced across her wings. Last year, there had been a massive Flying Exhibition, with obstacle courses and prizes for the best fliers. What would they do this year?

'We've decided to do something a bit different this time.' Miss Shimmery's blue eyes held a slight twinkle. 'Each year is to decide for itself what sort of exhibition you'd like to put on for your parents. It can be anything you like, but you're to be responsible for every aspect of it. Then, when the parents come, there will be prizes for the best work.'

An enthusiastic buzz swept the Branch. The Peony table exchanged eager glances. A whole exhibition that they planned themselves!

'And now, I think it's time to eat,' smiled Miss Shimmery. She raised an arm. 'Butterflies commence!'

As she drifted back down to the platform, the school's butterflies fluttered into the Great Branch, carrying oak-leaf platters piled high with seed cakes and fizzy nectar. A bright blue butterfly served the Peony table, dipping its wings gracefully.

Twink slowly helped herself to a cake. All around her, the others were talking excitedly to Kiki, telling her about last year's exhibition.

'How exciting!' breathed Kiki. 'We never did anything like that at Emerald Leaf. Everyone was too busy seeing who could be the snobbiest.'

The other girls laughed.

'And Twink won the prize for best flier in the school,' put in Sooze. 'Didn't she, Mariella?' She smiled innocently at the pointy-faced fairy, who had been extremely miffed that *she* hadn't won the prize. Mariella made a face at her.

'*Did* you, Twink? That's fantastic!' Kiki's smile was wide and genuine. 'Your parents must have been really proud.'

'Mm, I suppose,' muttered Twink. *Oh, stop pretending to be so nice,* she wanted to shout. *You don't care at all, really!*

Suddenly she realised that the others were staring at her. Bimi looked stricken, and Kiki had a hurt, puzzled frown on her face. 'Anyway, let's talk about *this* year,' Twink said quickly. 'What are we going to do?'

To her relief, they all started talking and swapping ideas and the moment passed. But that evening in the second-year wash branch, Bimi came over as Twink was scrubbing her arms with a mossy sponge.

'Twink, what's up with you?' Her pretty face was

flushed and upset. 'You were so rude to Kiki at dinner tonight!'

'I wasn't rude.' Twink concentrated on her washing, not looking up.

'You *were*,' insisted Bimi. 'She was only trying to be nice!'

'Well, who asked her to?' burst out Twink. She threw her sponge into a bucket with a splash. 'You seem so – so *entranced* with her, Bimi. Just because she's new, and has a famous mother!'

Bimi's mouth dropped open. She closed it with a snap. 'That has nothing to do with it! She's *nice*, that's all. Twink, why are you acting this way?'

'What way?' Twink met Bimi's gaze with a scowl. Across the branch, she could hear the shrieks and splashes of a water fight going on, and Sooze shouting, 'Take that!'

'Like –' Bimi stopped suddenly. Her wings went still as she peered at Twink. 'You're *jealous*,' she said in amazement. 'Just because I've made a new friend!'

Oh, so they were *friends* already! Twink grabbed a peppermint twig from the rack on the wall. 'I am not! I don't care *who* you're friends with – only I think you could choose someone a little better than Kiki, that's all.'

'What's wrong with Kiki?' The look of surprise on Bimi's face was almost comical.

'What isn't!' cried Twink. Her voice trembled. 'She puts on this act of being all humble and nice, but you can *tell* how much she loves being the centre of attention. It's sickening the way you were all fawning over her at dinner. And she was lapping up every second of it, too!'

Bimi stared at her, her blue eyes wide. Twink turned away and rubbed her teeth with the twig, glaring into the dewdrop mirror. Deep down, she knew she was being unreasonable, but she couldn't help it. Was she supposed to *like* Kiki, when the new girl was stealing her best friend?

'You know, Twink, this is really unfair.' Bimi sounded close to tears. 'It's perfectly all right for you to go off with Sooze whenever you feel like it, but if *I* have another friend, you get your wings all in a twist!' She flitted out of the branch, her silver and gold wings flashing in the steam.

Twink stared at her reflection in the walnut-shell bucket. It was true that she'd gone off with Sooze on occasion, but that had been different – Sooze had never tried to steal Bimi's best friend, the way Kiki was doing!

And besides, it's true what I said, she thought sullenly. Anyone with eyes in their head could see that Kiki loved being fussed over. Wringing out her sponge, Twink threw it in the bucket. Her reflection vanished in a splash.

The fairies were still talking eagerly about the exhibition the next afternoon in the second-year Common Branch – a long, comfortable branch filled with cosy mushroom seats and desks. A cluster of fire rocks sat at its centre, giving off a welcome heat in the autumn chill.

'We want ours to be the most glimmery exhibition ever!' said Jax, a fairy with spiky green hair from another branch. 'We've got to show those Third Years that we're the best.' She pounded her fist into her hand.

Lola, her best friend, nodded. 'How about a fairy cabaret?' she suggested brightly.

'No, let's do a play!' shouted someone else.

'But what if you can't act?' pointed out Pix. She was sitting perched on the fire rocks, writing down everyone's ideas in a petal pad. 'I think we should do something that includes everyone.'

Twink sat to one side with Sooze and Sili, trying to look interested as everyone called out suggestions. All the girls from Peony Branch were dressed in their new peony petal uniforms, made for them that morning by Mrs Hover. Bimi's and Kiki's dresses were the exact same shade of pink, noted Twink glumly.

The two fairies sat together near the fire rocks, their wings almost touching. Bimi was obviously avoiding Twink – they'd hardly spoken since the scene in the wash branch the night before. Twink grimaced and looked away. Fine, let her be that way if she wanted!

'*I've* got an idea!' cried Mariella suddenly. The

other fairies looked at her in surprise. Mariella hardly ever joined in – she usually sat sneering on the sidelines. But now her pointed face was flushed with excitement.

'It's perfect!' she went on. 'We'll have a fairy fashion show – and Kiki can be in charge, because she knows all about it!'

Chapter Four

A fashion show! An enthusiastic murmur swept through the Common Branch.

'*Nobody* else will be doing that,' said Jax with satisfaction. 'I vote yes! But why does Kiki get to be in charge?'

'Because her mother –' Mariella faltered when she saw the warning look on Sooze's face.

'What about her mother?' asked Jax in bewilderment.

'I think Mariella should be in charge,' put in Kiki quickly, her cheeks on fire. 'It was her idea.'

'*Mosquito Nose?*' Sooze gaped at Kiki in horror. 'You don't know what you're saying!'

'Kiki, why don't you just tell everyone?' suggested Bimi in an undertone. 'No one will treat you differently; we're not like that here.'

Ha! Twink pulled her knees up to her chin, hugging herself. And of course Kiki *would* tell everyone, she thought. She could probably hardly wait!

'Well . . . all right,' said Kiki. She took a deep breath and addressed the branch. 'My mother's a fashion designer, that's all. And she used to be a model. So I suppose I *do* know a little bit about fashion shows, but –'

'Her mother's Mirabel Moonglow!' burst out Mariella. She shot up into the air, bobbing up and down. 'She's in all the petal mags, she's really, really famous, and –'

'And we're NOT GOING TO MAKE A FUSS ABOUT IT,' bellowed Sooze, standing up and propping her hands on her hips. '*Are* we, Mosquito Nose?'

Mariella drifted back to the floor again. 'No,' she said sulkily, folding her wings behind her back. 'I was just saying, that's all.'

'But Kiki, that's great!' Jax scraped her hands excitedly through her short green hair. 'You'll know everything we should do – of *course* you should be in charge.'

'But I don't *want* to be in charge!' Kiki fluttered her wings in alarm. 'I've only just got here!'

'Well, what better way to get to know everyone?' said Pix with a grin. 'I think Jax is right, Kiki.'

Enthusiastic agreement echoed through the branch.

'Oh, Kiki, *please* say yes!'

'We wouldn't know what to do!'

'I bet you've got loads of brilliant ideas!'

'Well . . .' Kiki hesitated, looking flustered. She glanced at Bimi, who gave her an encouraging smile. 'I've always liked watching my mum work . . . and I suppose I *do* have a few ideas for how we could put a show together . . .'

'Hurrah!' burst out Sooze. She shot up in the air

and did a somersault, her pink wings flashing. 'We'll have the best exhibition ever!'

'But I'll need an assistant,' said Kiki. 'There's going to be loads to do!'

'I'll be your assistant,' offered Bimi. 'I'd love to help!'

'Bimi, you can't just be an *assistant*!' cried Sooze. 'You're the prettiest fairy in our year – you have to be one of the models.'

Twink saw a hint of longing shine in Bimi's eyes, and then a rush of pure panic. Bimi shook her head quickly. 'No, not me! Being Kiki's assistant sounds glimmery.'

'I think so, too,' said Kiki warmly. 'We'll have loads of fun working together, Bimi.'

As the rest of the branch clustered around Kiki, Twink bit her lip to hold back the tears. It was even worse than she had seen in the crystal. Now Bimi and Kiki would be spending all of their time together, making plans and having fun. Soon Bimi would probably forget that she and Twink had ever been friends at all.

'Twink, what are you doing over here on your own?' asked Pix, flitting over to her. 'Isn't a fashion show a great idea? I can hardly wait to see what Kiki comes up with!'

'Yeah, great,' said Twink curtly. 'Anyway, I'm sure Kiki will love all the attention.' She grabbed up her things. She couldn't bear to stay here another moment! 'I'm going to bed now,' she announced, and flew from the branch as fast as she could.

Behind her, Pix exchanged an amazed glance with Sili and Zena. 'What's wrong with *her*?' asked

Sili, her eyes wide.

Pix shook her head, staring after Twink. 'I don't know, but I hope she snaps out of it soon. She's acting like she hates everybody!'

'Autumn is a very important time,' said Miss Petal, leaning against her mushroom desk. 'It's when the trees discard their old leaves and prepare themselves for winter. But fallen leaves aren't just pretty to look at.'

Twink sat with her chin slumped on her hand as their Flower Power teacher took a red oak leaf from the bark cupboard. Near the front of the branch, Bimi and Kiki sat together. *Naturally*, thought Twink. The two of them were practically inseparable these days.

Miss Petal manoeuvred the large leaf on to her mushroom desk. Its edges draped over the sides. 'Now, who can tell me how we use fallen leaves to take care of trees?'

As usual, Pix's hand shot into the air. 'Fallen leaves contain the histories of their trees,' she said. 'So you can find out everything about the tree they fell from, if you know how to read them.'

'That's right,' smiled Miss Petal. 'Now, who knows . . .'

Twink's thoughts drifted to the fashion show. Plans for it had been going on for weeks now, and it was all the Second Year could talk about.

Kiki's first idea had been that every fairy should design her own outfit, but the others had protested. 'No, *you* should do it,' said Sooze, to a chorus of agreement. 'I couldn't design an outfit worth a pebble, but I bet you'd be great at it!'

A shy smile had lit up Kiki's face. 'Well . . . I'd love to, but only if everyone's really sure . . .'

And of course everyone had insisted, thought Twink sourly. So Kiki had been busily designing outfits for them all, and now, for the last few days, there had been frequent flashes of fairy dust as she and her helpers began to make them. Everyone was dying to see their dresses, but Kiki insisted that they were a secret until they were all ready.

And now they were. Kiki had got permission for the Second Years to practise in the Great Branch that evening, and they were going to have their first rehearsal.

I can hardly wait, groaned Twink to herself, propping her chin on her hand. *Kiki will be showing off as usual, and Bimi acting like she's the most wonderful fairy ever . . .*

She started as Sili nudged her.

'. . . Twink, would you come and demonstrate how to read the tree's history?' Miss Petal was saying.

Twink gulped as everyone turned to look at her. Oh no! What had she missed?

'Well?' Miss Petal looked quizzically at her.

Slowly, Twink flitted to the front of the branch. The red leaf seemed to be smirking at her. Perhaps if she just touched it, and tried to hear its history in her mind? A lot of fairy magic was like that – it was worth a try, anyway!

Twink rested her hands on the leaf and closed her eyes. *Tell me about the tree you fell from,* she thought.

A snigger ran through the branch. Twink's cheeks caught fire as she opened her eyes. Miss Petal was

tapping her wings together.

'You weren't listening to a word I said, were you?' she chided. 'You have to stroke the leaf's *veins* to get its history.' She ran her fingers along the veins that criss-crossed the leaf's surface. 'Just touching it won't do anything at all!'

Twink's wings felt stiff. She couldn't look at the others. Oh, *why* did Kiki have to be sitting right there, watching? She must be loving this!

'Zena, come and show us, please,' said Miss Petal. 'And Twink, remember that you can't make assumptions about magic. It doesn't always do what you expect, so you need to do your research.'

Twink slunk back to her mushroom as Zena flew to the front of the branch. Bimi gave her a sidelong glance and then looked away again, tossing her hair.

She acts like she's glad to be rid of me, now that she's got her new best friend, thought Twink. Tears stung her eyes as she scribbled notes in her petal pad, hardly noticing what she was writing. Oh, why did the crystal have to have been so *right*?

Suddenly she sat up with a gasp. What was it Miss

Petal had said? *Don't make assumptions.* Yet that was exactly what she'd been doing. She'd assumed that the crystal had to be right, but – but what if it were possible to reverse its fortune somehow, so that she and Bimi were best friends again? Hadn't Miss Petal just said she had to do her research?

That's it. I have to find out everything I can about crystals, thought Twink fervently. Fidgeting with impatience, she glanced out of the window, counting the minutes until the lesson ended and she could get to the library.

After dinner that evening the second-year fairies stayed behind in the Great Branch, getting ready for their rehearsal. Kiki flew overhead, shouting directions. 'Let's move these tables against the walls, so that we have a nice long space down the middle. Yes, that's right! Glimmery!'

Twink helped with the others, though it irritated her to be taking orders from Kiki. She thought she was so wonderful, just because of her famous mum! *Why* couldn't the others see how vain she was?

But no one else seemed to. When the tables were arranged to Kiki's satisfaction, the fairies drifted to the centre of the Great Branch, chattering and laughing. 'I can hardly wait to see what she's designed for us,' said Zena, her eyes shining. 'Did you see? She's got a whole pile of dresses with her!'

'Mm,' said Twink.

She glanced at her petal bag, which sat with a pile of fairies' belongings against the wall. She'd found three books on crystal magic at the library, and was aching to have a look at them. If only she didn't

have to take part in the rehearsal!

Zena let out a breath. 'Twink, what's wrong with you, anyway?' she burst out. 'You're so grumpy this term! You're no fun at all any more – everyone's noticed it.'

'What?' Twink stared at her, startled out of her thoughts. 'I'm not grumpy!'

But Zena had already flown away, and was talking to Jax and Lola halfway across the branch. Twink stood by herself, feeling cross and out of sorts. Was it true that everyone was talking about her?

'But that's so unfair,' she murmured, clenching her fists. Kiki was the one who had come into their branch, disrupting everything! Why didn't they gossip about *her*?

'Talking to yourself again, Opposite?' asked a voice behind her.

Sooze! Twink whirled towards her in relief.

'Sooze, you won't believe what Zena just said,' she cried. 'She said everyone's talking about me, and that I'm no fun any more!' Twink waited indignantly for her friend's response.

Sooze raised a lavender eyebrow, looking amused.

'What?' asked Twink, a chill of dread settling between her wings. 'Don't – don't you think she's being really unfair?'

Sooze shrugged. 'No, actually I think she let you off pretty lightly. You've been acting like a real thistle head this term, Twink. Everyone's saying they don't blame Bimi for liking Kiki better.'

Oh! Twink gaped at Sooze. It felt like she had been slapped. Sudden tears stung at her eyes, and her chin trembled.

Sooze pulled a face. 'Oh, dry up, Twink! It can't be as bad as all that – just stop acting like a grumbling gremlin. Now come on, let's go and see what our dresses are like!' And she flitted off towards the platform, where Kiki was getting ready to speak to the excited crowd of Second Years.

Chapter Five

Twink followed Sooze in a daze. Nobody understood at all. Standing on the edge of the crowd, she glared up at the platform where Kiki stood. This was all *her* fault, not Twink's!

'Is everyone ready to get started?' Kiki's wings tapped together nervously as the Second Years fell into an expectant silence. Bimi stood beside her, holding a pile of flowery dresses.

Now that the moment of unveiling had arrived, Kiki looked very unsure of herself. 'Right, I've got the dresses ready – and, um, I really hope you like them. I tried to plan outfits that would suit you all. I mean, go with your hair colour and wing colour, and . . . um, personality . . .' she trailed off, biting her lip.

'Get on with it!' called Sooze. The others laughed good-naturedly.

Kiki's wings relaxed as she grinned. 'All right, you asked for it!' she called back. 'Sooze, this is yours.'

She had a quick rummage in the pile Bimi was holding, and whipped out a bright purple dress with a broad zig-zag streak of hot pink across its front. The Second Year gasped in delight.

'Sooze, it's perfect for you!' squealed Sili, clapping her hands.

Sooze flitted on to the platform and held the dress up in front of her. It was very short, with a high neck and long, fluttery sleeves.

'I love it!' cried Sooze, bouncing on her toes. 'Kiki, you're a genius!' She danced off to the changing area that Kiki had set up behind a screen of oak leaves, and a moment later emerged resplendent.

Soon the other fairies were exclaiming in delight as well. They all seemed to have outfits that were perfect for them. Pix was in a simple, stylish dress of daisy petals; Sili in sparkly silver shorts and a shimmering turquoise top. Even Mariella looked wonderful, in a pale orchid dress with gauzy green sleeves.

It was impossible not to feel swept up in the excitement, and soon Twink's heart was beating faster with every name called. What had Kiki designed for her? Perhaps something pink, to go with her hair – made from rose petals, maybe . . .

'Twink, here's yours,' called Kiki.

A hush fell as Twink flew up to the platform. Most of the Second Year were aware of the tension between the two fairies, and Twink's pointed ears burned as she realised that everyone was watching.

Kiki smiled uncertainly as Twink landed in front of her. 'I – I wanted to do something special for you, Twink – something that no one else could wear.'

Twink felt a flutter of apprehension. Nobody else had had this sort of speech. What on earth had Kiki designed for her?

Slowly, Kiki took one of the remaining dresses from Bimi. 'Um . . . here it is,' she said, offering it to Twink.

Twink stared in horror at the thing Kiki was holding out to her. It was a short tunic made from prickly dandelion leaves, with splashes of blue and gold paint making wild patterns over it. A spiky green cap made from a horse-chestnut shell went with it.

'Do you like it?' asked Kiki anxiously. 'I just thought – you have such interesting looks, Twink; and it takes someone with real personality to carry off a dress like this . . .' she faltered as she saw the expression on Twink's face.

'Yes, it's great,' said Twink coolly.

She took the dress from Kiki, wincing as one of the dandelion spikes jabbed her in the arm. What was 'interesting looks' supposed to mean? And 'real personality' . . . ha! Obviously, Kiki was making

Twink wear this hideous dress so that everyone would laugh at her.

'I hope the *inside* isn't dandelion leaves,' said Twink. The entire Second Year was nudging each other and whispering.

'Oh, no!' Kiki reassured her. Her purple eyes looked worried. 'It's dandelion fluff; really nice and soft. Try it on – it'll look great on you, I promise!'

Had Bimi been in on this as well? Twink gave her

a hard look, but Bimi was busy with another fairy, studiously avoiding Twink's gaze.

Close to tears, Twink flew behind the oak-leaf screen and pulled on the dress. Adjusting the thorny cap on her head, she stared in the small dewdrop mirror. She looked like an exploded dandelion, with ugly spikes sticking out every which way!

'Ooh, *Twink*,' breathed Sili. 'Is that your outfit? I've never seen anything like it!'

'Who has?' snapped Twink. She pulled at the dress, and then jerked her hand away as the spikes pricked her palm. *Oh!* That awful Kiki – she was probably having a good snigger, right at this very moment!

'Yes, but it really suits you.' Sili was flying slowly around Twink, taking her in from every angle. 'It looks so *different* – it's really something!'

Twink made a face. Sili was so scatty that she'd think anything looked good. Or, worse yet, maybe she was in on the prank with Kiki and Bimi. Maybe the whole branch was, to get back at Twink for being such a *thistle head*. They were all blaming her,

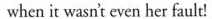

when it wasn't even her fault!

Twink's pulse pounded hotly. She flitted out from behind the screen and joined the crowd of Second Years. She half hoped that someone would make a comment about her dress, just so she could snarl at them!

But no one seemed to notice her. Suddenly Twink realised that everyone's attention was on the platform, where Kiki and Bimi seemed to be having a row.

'Because I knew you'd just say no if I mentioned it before!' said Kiki, flapping her wings in exasperation. 'Sooze was right, Bimi – you *have* to be a model. You're the prettiest fairy in the whole year!'

Twink thought Bimi looked terrified, in spite of her secret longing to follow in her mother's wing strokes. 'No, no, I don't want to!' she said, backing away. 'Really, I'm happy just being an assistant behind the scenes.'

Kiki sighed. 'Well, at least let me show you the outfit I made for you.'

She drew a dress out from a hidden place behind the platform. A gasp rippled across the Second

Years. It was a long, sleeveless gown of dark blue iris petals, with silver and gold stars shimmering across it like the most magical night sky imaginable.

'Oh,' whispered Bimi. As if in a dream, she fluttered slowly forward, touching the soft petal fabric. 'Kiki, it's – it's beautiful.'

'Then you'll wear it?' asked Kiki eagerly. 'Oh, Bimi, please say yes. It'll look gorgeous on you!'

Bimi swallowed hard, obviously deeply torn. 'I . . . but then I'd have to model it in front of everyone . . .'

'Well, yes, that's the idea,' laughed Kiki. She swayed the dress enticingly. 'Oh, come on, Bimi – why not *enjoy* being pretty for a change?'

Twink watched as Bimi bit her lip, staring at the dress. The little stars shimmered and twinkled. 'All right, I'll do it!' she burst out.

The Second Year burst into cheers, beating their wings together. Bimi's cheeks blazed bright red. Grabbing the dress from Kiki, she flitted behind the screen. A few moments later, she edged out from behind it.

'Um . . . how do I look?' she asked, her face still on fire.

Twink blinked. Bimi looked beautiful, of course – but her expression was so terrified that it ruined the effect of the dress. She looked as if a swarm of angry wasps had forced her to put it on, and were ready to sting her if she didn't get it right!

'Gorgeous,' said Kiki firmly. 'And you'll look even

more gorgeous when you're feeling more relaxed. Now come on, everyone, let's practise how to move down the flyway like a real model. Ready?'

'Wait,' cried Sooze, hovering in her purple dress. 'First, let's give three cheers for Mariella, for thinking of the fashion show in the first place!'

As the Second Years chorused an enthusiastic round of cheers, the pointy-faced fairy's cheeks blushed a deep crimson. 'Thank you!' she gasped. For once, Twink thought, she'd completely forgotten to act superior!

'Right, everyone, let's practise our moves,' called Kiki when they had finished. 'Just do what I do.'

Twink flew with the others, trying to imitate Kiki's effortless glide and graceful poses. It was harder than it looked, especially in a dress she hated. Twink's arms and legs felt like awkward sticks that refused to do what she asked.

Kiki flitted among the girls, arranging them in pairs. 'Sooze, you fly with Lola . . . Mariella, you and Pix should go together . . .'

She hesitated when she got to Twink. 'Um . . . Twink, I think you should fly on your own. Your dress is one of a kind – I want to really show it off!'

'Fine,' said Twink tightly. She might have known that Kiki would make her go alone, just to embarrass her even more.

Finally the fairies gathered on the sidelines, whispering excitedly as they waited to begin their first fly-through. Sooze and Lola went first. Propping her hands on her hips, Sooze put on a dramatically pouty model's face as she flew, whirling this way and that as if she were born to it.

'Go, Sooze!' shouted Sili, clapping her hands.

Even Lola looked like she was having fun, posing shyly in her bright green sparkle-dress. Fairy after fairy flew down the Branch, all of them radiant in their beautiful outfits. By the time it was Twink's turn, she was more conscious than ever of how awful she looked.

'Ready, Twink?' Kiki was hovering to one side, taking notes on a petal pad.

Scowling, Twink took off down the length of the

Great Branch. Belatedly, she remembered that she was supposed to be posing, and put her arms stiffly out to her sides.

Stifled laughter rippled across the Second Years. 'Come on, Opposite, can't you look a bit crosser?' called out Sooze. Flinging her arms out, Sooze gave a ferocious mock scowl. The Branch erupted into howls of merriment.

Twink hovered in place, trembling with embarrassed fury. How dare they all laugh at her! She saw Kiki bite back a smile, too, and suddenly the weeks of pent-up emotion burst out of her like an earthquake.

Snatching the cap off her head, Twink threw it to the floor. 'Shut up!' she shouted. The Second Years stopped laughing and stared at her.

'Shut up, all of you! I'm *not* wearing this stupid, ugly dress. In fact – in fact, I'm not even going to *be* in the fashion show, so you can all find someone else to laugh at!'

'Oh, *Twink* –' started Kiki.

Twink didn't wait. Jetting back behind the

oak-leaf screen, she flung off the horrible dress and struggled back into her uniform. Then, pausing only to grab her bag from the pile on the floor, she flew out of the Great Branch as fast as she could.

Chapter
Six

Crystal magic takes place in many ways. One of the most common is to take an appropriate crystal (for instance, rose quartz for love, amethyst for inspiration, etc.) and cast a corresponding spell upon it. The crystal then acts to strengthen the spell, and also provides a handy talisman. This is especially useful when . . .

Twink groaned and flipped a page. This book was just the same as the other two had been. Pages and pages about how to use crystals for fairy magic, but not a single word about how to reverse a crystal prophecy!

Twink looked up, and realised she was alone in the second-year Common Branch.

She sighed and stretched her wings.

And now she needed such advice more than ever. Ever since Twink's outburst in the Great Branch several weeks before, the entire Second Year seemed to be avoiding her. Kiki had given the dandelion-leaf dress to Jax to wear, and told Twink that she could work on the lights for the fashion show, if she preferred.

'And Twink,' she started to add, rubbing her purple wings together fretfully. 'I didn't mean – that is, I –'

But Twink had only stared stonily at her, until Kiki finally gave up and turned away.

So now Twink was working the glow-worm lights, high up in the rafters. She tickled the worms' tummies to turn them on and off, and put bright crystal panels in front of the lanterns to change the spotlights into different colours.

It wasn't terribly exciting work, and Twink spent long hours watching the models practise with her

chin propped on her hand. Nobody even seemed to remember that she was up there, and she felt very alone.

At the same time, the fashion show was really starting to come together. The second-year fairies were gaining in confidence more and more as the days went on, sashaying down the flyway like real models. Even Lola was skimming about stylishly now, looking almost as sure of herself as Sooze.

The only one who didn't seem to be having fun was Jax, who complained that she wasn't the 'type' to model. 'This really isn't my thing,' she muttered once, as she struck a pose. 'How do models keep from being bored to death?'

But the biggest surprise of all was Bimi. The blue-haired fairy had grimaced nervously the first few times she practised her moves, flying almost as stiffly as Twink had done. Yet bit by bit, she was clearly starting to enjoy herself. Just the day before, Twink had watched, open-mouthed, as Bimi flitted gracefully down the flyway, executing a series of midair pirouettes that made the stars on her dress flash like diamonds.

'Bimi, that's great!' Kiki shouted as the other girls burst into applause.

'It wasn't bad, was it?' Bimi smiled broadly, her expression radiant.

Twink had stared down from the rafters in amazement. Instead of blushing and ducking her head shyly, Bimi actually seemed pleased by the attention. She held her head higher than usual as she flitted back to the changing screen, and flipped her hair back in a very un-Bimi-like way.

Then, later that night, Bimi and Kiki had talked about fashion for ages, decorating each other's wings with a special glittery polish. Trying to read one of her books on crystals hidden inside a petal mag, Twink had watched in horrified amazement. Bimi had *never* decorated her wings before! What was happening to her?

Now, in the second-year Common Branch, Twink stared down at the useless books in frustration. *I've got to find some way to reverse the prophecy soon,* she thought miserably. *Or else it'll be too late, and Bimi*

will be gone for good.

Stacking the three books together, Twink took them back to the Glitterwings library. Mrs Stamen was at her mushroom desk, surrounded by high shelves that touched the ceiling. It was very quiet, with only a few girls flitting about the highest shelves, far overhead.

'Did you find what you needed?' asked Mrs Stamen, checking the books in with a snail-trail pen.

Twink sighed. 'Not really,' she admitted.

The librarian looked at the spine of one of the petal books. '*Crystal Magic*,' she read in surprise. 'No, we don't have many books on crystals, I'm afraid – it's a very specialised field. But you could always ask Miss Sparkle if you have any questions about them.'

Twink blinked. 'Miss *Sparkle*? But she teaches Fairy Dust!'

Mrs Stamen nodded as she turned away to help another student. 'Yes, but she's made quite a study of crystals – there's probably not much about them that she doesn't know.'

Mrs Stamen

'Thanks, Mrs Stamen,' murmured Twink.

Flying out of the library, Twink bit her lip thoughtfully as she headed back towards Peony Branch. The dour second-year head wasn't Twink's favourite teacher, and the thought of telling her about the awful fortune she had seen wasn't very tempting. She'd probably just tell Twink she had been a moss brain to look in the crystal in the first place!

Suddenly Twink started. Bimi and Kiki were drifting down the trunk towards her, deep in conversation. Without thinking, Twink ducked into a knothole. The two fairies stopped nearby, hovering and chatting.

'How do you think I should do my hair?' Bimi was saying. 'Should I wear it up in a ponytail, maybe with some dewdrop ornaments?'

'Maybe,' said Kiki. 'Or you could just wear it long, with little sparkles sprinkled in it!'

'Ooh, silver and gold, to match my wings!' cried Bimi. 'I could even sprinkle some on my arms – wouldn't that look glimmery?'

Twink made a face. *What* had come over Bimi? She sounded exactly like one of those silly fairies from the upper years, who only cared about wing polish and making their petal skirts shorter. She'd be swooning over boy fairies next!

'Oh, Kiki, I never thought I'd actually be a model!' Bimi's blue eyes shone. 'And in such a gorgeous dress, too. You're doing a great job on the show, you know. Everyone's having a brilliant time.'

'Except for Twink, I suppose.' Kiki pushed her lilac curls back with a sigh. 'I really feel awful that

I've come between the two of you, Bimi.'

Twink stiffened. She hadn't realised that Kiki knew about their friendship – Bimi must have told her.

'Well, it's not *your* fault,' said Bimi. 'I tried talking to her over and over again, but she was just impossible. I've really had enough of her this term, Kiki. She's changed completely!'

Still talking, the two fairies flew away. Twink felt icy cold, and then a searing heat blazed through her. How could Bimi say that *she* had changed, when Bimi was the one suddenly going on about wing polish and hairstyles?

And now . . . and now Bimi had had enough of her. The heat left Twink in a rush as she struggled against tears. It was too late, then. There was nothing she could do.

'No!' she decided suddenly, clenching her fists. Spiralling quickly up the trunk, Twink dodged past a crowd of older girls and landed, breathing hard, on the ledge outside Miss Sparkle's branch. She knocked.

'Come in,' called a voice.

Miss Sparkle was sitting at her mushroom desk, marking petal papers. She looked up as Twink flitted in. 'Yes?'

Twink's throat was dry. 'I just wondered if I could ask you something,' she blurted. 'About – about crystals. Mrs Stamen said that you'd made a study of them.'

Miss Sparkle raised an eyebrow. 'Yes, that's right,' she said drily. 'Why do you need to know about crystals?'

'I – I just do,' said Twink. 'It's really important.' She held her breath, half expecting Miss Sparkle to tell her off for wasting her time.

Instead Miss Sparkle considered Twink for a long moment, and then nodded. 'Come to see me after breakfast tomorrow,' she said, standing up and shuffling the petals together. 'You can ask me whatever you like then.'

'Boring,' said Sooze.

Kiki looked exasperated. 'Sooze, we've been over

and over this. There's going to be glimmery music playing, and different-coloured lights – we don't *need* anything else.'

Twink undressed for bed mechanically, barely listening to the argument. A knot twisted in her stomach at the thought of her meeting with Miss Sparkle the next morning. What if the Fairy Dust teacher couldn't help her after all?

'But lights and music are so ordinary,' insisted Sooze, pulling on her thistle-down dressing gown. 'We need something different. Like – like an explosion of fairy dust flares! Something to make everyone sit up and take notice!'

'That's what the *dresses* are supposed to do,' groaned Kiki. 'If you have fairy dust flares going off all over the place, nobody will even notice them.'

'I think Kiki's right,' commented Zena, polishing her orange wings. 'The dresses are glimmery enough – we don't need lots of flash and sparkle.'

'That's what I think, too,' said Bimi. Twink had noticed that she spoke up much more often these days, eager to put her opinion in. 'We put Kiki in charge, Sooze, so let's do what she says. She knows all about fashion shows.'

A ripple of assent ran across the branch. 'Besides, fairy dust flares might smudge the dresses,' pointed out Mariella. 'Especially if *you're* in charge of them, Sooze.'

Sooze huffed out an irritated breath. 'Honestly, you're all so boring! If you'd just let me *try* it, then you'd see –'

'*No*, Sooze,' laughed Pix. 'The majority has spoken! Now come on, it's time for lights out – Mrs Hover will be up in a minute.'

The fairies chatted to each other as they climbed into their mossy beds. Twink pulled her petal duvet up around her pointed ears. No one paid any attention to her, or even appeared to notice her silence.

Her other friends had had enough of her, too, it seemed. They were used to her being an outsider now – someone who kept to herself, and didn't join in.

But maybe that's all going to change, thought Twink, screwing her eyes tightly shut. *Maybe Miss*

Sparkle can give me a crystal spell that will put things right again. Oh, I hope she can!

The next morning after breakfast, Twink knocked shyly on Miss Sparkle's door. 'Come in,' the voice called again. This time Miss Sparkle sat waiting as Twink entered, her white wings folded neatly behind her back.

'Take a mushroom,' she said, motioning. 'Now, what do you need to know?'

Twink sat down, feeling very small suddenly. She took a deep breath. 'Well – you see, I – I stayed with Bimi over the last holidays, and –' Haltingly, her story came out: going to the crystal caverns, what Bimi's father had said, and how she had sneaked back to look into the mysterious crystal.

Miss Sparkle raised an eyebrow. 'You shouldn't trust crystal visions, Twink. They're not very reliable.'

Twink's eyes widened. 'But it *was* reliable!' she cried. 'It showed me awful things, and they've *all* come true.' Choking over the words, she told her year head exactly what she had seen. Her cheeks burned as she described the images of Bimi and Kiki.

Something almost like a smile crossed Miss Sparkle's face. 'That's exactly what I mean. Those sorts of crystals are called trickster crystals, Twink. You see, it didn't show you what *had* to be – it showed you what *might* be, but only because you were foolish enough to look into it in the first place.'

Twink bit her lip in bewilderment. 'I don't –'

Miss Sparkle shook her head. 'My dear, it's very simple. If you *hadn't* looked into the crystal, what would have happened when Kiki came to school?'

'I . . . I don't know,' said Twink. She tried to think. 'I suppose I would have wanted to help her at first, the same as Bimi. But she's awfully stuck up, even if the others can't see it . . .' she faltered under her year head's keen stare.

'*Is* she?' Miss Sparkle demanded. 'Or is that just what you think because you looked into the crystal, and felt jealous of her before you even met her?'

Miss Sparkle's words struck Twink like a lightning bolt. She thought of Kiki's wide smile, and bright, friendly eyes. Suddenly she felt like an idiot.

'I – I suppose she's not *really* stuck-up,' she mumbled. 'But –'

'But nothing!' said Miss Sparkle briskly. 'You see, if you hadn't looked into the crystal in the first place, you'd probably have liked Kiki, and you all could have been friends – isn't that right?'

Twink gaped at Miss Sparkle, her mind spinning. It was true! Even Bimi's new preoccupation with her looks might have seemed different, if Twink hadn't been so convinced that Kiki was Bimi's new best friend. Oh, how could she have been so stupid?

The year head smiled wryly. 'And what did Bimi's father say? That the crystal would show you what would happen – *if* you looked into it? He knew as well, you see. Trickster crystals can be so convincing that you often *make* the event come about, just by believing in it. But Twink, nothing at all can happen unless you let it. You're in charge of your destiny, not a crystal!'

'Oh, but – but that means . . .' Twink trailed off as a memory of how she'd been acting all term swept over her: keeping to herself, growling when the other fairies spoke to her, only taking part in their activities when she had to.

No wonder everyone had been avoiding her! And Bimi – why, Twink couldn't blame her for becoming so fed up. She'd been acting like a complete moss brain!

'Is there anything else, Twink?' asked Miss Sparkle gently.

'No,' murmured Twink. She got to her feet in a daze. 'I mean – I mean, *thank* you!' she burst out as relief rushed through her. 'Oh, Miss Sparkle, thank you so much!'

Unexpectedly, Miss Sparkle smiled. Escorting Twink to the door, she touched her shoulder. 'Not at all, Twink. But next time, you might try listening when someone tells you not to do something!'

Chapter
Seven

Twink stood on the sidelines in the Great Branch, watching as the final rehearsal for the fashion show started. 'Right, everyone, let's go!' called Kiki, hovering overhead.

The Branch plunged into darkness. On the platform, the school's cricket band started up a jazzy tune as Sooze and Lola appeared, lit by dramatic white spotlights. They swished through the air, hands on hips, as the lights changed to green and blue. Up above, Jax sat in the rafters working the glow-worms, looking like she was enjoying herself at last.

Twink glanced down and adjusted her hemline, taking care not to touch the prickles. She was wearing the dandelion-leaf dress, and the spiky cap was set at a rakish angle on her head.

'You look great!' whispered Sili, bobbing in the air beside her. The silver-haired fairy tucked her arm through Twink's with a friendly squeeze. 'And Twink, I'm so glad you're yourself again!'

Twink grinned at her sheepishly. 'Me, too,' she whispered back.

After her meeting with Miss Sparkle, Twink had apologised to Kiki that very morning after Dance class. Kiki's eyes had widened as Twink stumblingly explained what she'd seen in the crystal.

'Oh, you poor thing!' she breathed, touching Twink's arm. 'No *wonder* you hated me when we first met. I'd have felt exactly the same!'

'Then you forgive me?' Twink held her breath. The two fairies were hovering near the circle of spotted mushrooms where Dance class was held, the rest of Peony Branch having gone on ahead.

'Of course!' said Kiki warmly. 'I couldn't under-stand what I'd done to upset you – I'm just glad there was a reason for it!'

'Not much of one, I suppose.' Twink grimaced. 'I feel like such a moss brain, Kiki. I just hope Bimi will forgive me, too.'

'She will,' Kiki assured her. 'She's really missed you, Twink. She'll be thrilled to have her best friend back!'

The two fairies smiled at each other and started flying back to school in the cool autumn breeze. *She's so nice!* thought Twink, darting sideways to avoid a flurry of falling leaves. *Miss Sparkle was right – it was all in my head.*

Suddenly Kiki stopped. 'Twink, there's just one thing –' she broke off uncertainly.

'What?' asked Twink, hovering beside her.

Kiki hesitated. 'Well, it's just . . . would you mind wearing the dandelion-leaf dress in the show after all? It doesn't look right on Jax, and she's not having fun anyway. I made it with *you* in mind, Twink – I really think you're the only one who can carry it off!'

Twink had readily agreed, though secretly she still wasn't sure what she thought of the dress. But to her surprise, the next time she tried it on it looked very different than she remembered – its prickles seemed sophisticated and exotic, with the bold splashes of paint perfectly bringing out the colour of her hair and wings.

How could I have been so wrong? wondered Twink now, still waiting on the sidelines for her turn. Obviously, the grouchy mood she'd been in all term had made her see the dress differently, too. She shuddered. What a pain she must have been!

Out of the corner of her eye, she saw Bimi waiting as well, looking beautiful in her long blue gown. She sighed. If only Bimi had been as easy to apologise to as Kiki! But Twink had somehow messed things up badly, so that the two friends were as distant as ever.

The same day that she'd sorted things out with Kiki, Twink had got Bimi on her own in the second-year Common Branch. At first, Bimi had been as distressed as Kiki to learn about the crystal.

'Oh, Twink!' she cried. 'Is *that* what was wrong?

Why didn't you tell me?'

'I don't know . . . I just couldn't,' mumbled Twink. Stupidly, fresh tears sprang to her eyes. 'I just felt so awful about it. I hated the thought of you being best friends with someone else! And then later, when you seemed to change so much, I –'

Bimi stared at her. '*I* seemed to change? You mean *you* did.'

Twink nodded. 'I know, I acted really stupidly . . . but Bimi, *you* changed too – you know, always going on about fashion and your looks.'

Bimi stiffened. '*Going on* about it? What do you mean?'

Twink groped for words. 'Well – you're always doing your hair now, and talking about different kinds of wing polish, and you seem to really like everyone watching you in the show . . .' Twink trailed off. Bimi's face was ablaze with anger.

'So you think I'm acting stuck-up, is that it?' she snapped.

'No!' cried Twink. 'But – you know, you might

just be getting carried away with it all a tiny bit –'

She was talking to thin air. Bimi had flounced off to the other end of the Common Branch. Sitting at a mushroom desk, she banged open a petal pad and pointedly began her homework.

That had been over two weeks ago. Nothing Twink had said since had made any difference. Bimi remained cold towards Twink, and redoubled her efforts in the fashion show. She spent hours practising her moves, and fussed over her hair and wings each night until they gleamed.

Kiki, caught in the middle, was obviously torn. 'What am I supposed to do?' she said to Twink in exasperation. 'I like you both!'

At least the rest of Peony Branch was acting normally towards Twink again – now that she was acting normally herself! Hovering on the sidelines in the Great Branch, Twink watched the models sashay through the air, posing and pouting. They all looked like they were having a glimmery time. Bimi, preparing to go on, shook her dress out and touched her hair.

'Get ready, Opposite,' hissed a voice in Twink's ear. Twink glanced at Sooze in surprise.

'But it's not my turn yet,' she whispered back.

The lavender-haired fairy grinned. 'I mean, get ready for things to be livened up a bit!' Before Twink could demand to know what she was talking about, Sooze had flitted off.

Bimi, after a final check of her dress, took to the air. Its little stars shimmered in the spotlight as she turned this way and that with a confident smile. But no sooner had she started her series of pirouettes then a massive *BANG* burst through the Great Branch. And then another! And another!

Bimi screamed as a series of pink and gold explosions went off all around her. Sparks spat and spun, screeching about the Branch like crazed birds. The second-year fairies squealed and dived for cover. Bimi, panic-stricken, tried to dart through the bursts – but then the largest explosion yet went off right beside her, swallowing her up in pink and gold sparks.

'Bimi!' shouted Twink. Leaving the mossy table

she had taken refuge under, she swooped out to save her friend, doing a quick barrel roll to avoid a shower of hissing pink sparks.

'I'm sorry, I'm sorry!' shrieked Sooze to the Branch at large, wringing her hands. 'I didn't mean – it wasn't supposed to be like this –'

The Great Branch's doors slammed open. '*What* is going on?' bellowed Miss Sparkle. 'Girls! Who set off these fairy dust flares?'

Her words hung in the sudden silence as the final spark sizzled and died. The only other sound was that of sobbing. Bimi lay huddled on the floor of the Branch, covering her head. Twink knelt by her side, trying in vain to comfort her.

All of Bimi's beautiful blue hair had been singed off.

'Yes, we know you didn't *mean* to hurt anyone, Sooze,' sighed Pix that night in Peony Branch. 'But that doesn't help Bimi, does it? The poor thing's still down in the infirmary, trying to see if Mrs Hover can grow her hair back in time for the exhibition!'

Sooze scowled guiltily. 'Oh, it'll grow back in a few weeks anyway – I don't see why she's making *that* much of a fuss. And come on, everyone, wasn't it really sort of glimmery when the flares went off . . . ?'

There was a stony silence from the rest of the branch. 'All right, all right!' burst out Sooze. 'It wasn't glimmery at all; it was stupid of me. Anyway, I've been punished enough, so you can all stop having a go!'

Glowering, Sooze flopped on to her mossy bed. Watching her, Twink felt a twinge of sympathy. Miss Sparkle had written to Sooze's parents . . . but worse than that, she'd forbidden Sooze to use fairy dust for the rest of the school year. This would seriously affect her Seedling Exams the following term. With her Fairy Dust class as an 'incomplete', Sooze would have to work very hard for the rest of her marks to be high enough to pass.

Everyone looked up as Bimi flew into the branch. Her eyes were red from crying, and she wore a clover-leaf bonnet, covering her baldness. Without a word, she rushed to her bed and threw herself face downwards.

Twink crouched beside her, touching her shoulder. 'Bimi? What did Mrs Hover say?'

'She can't do anything,' came Bimi's muffled voice. 'It has to grow back on its own. Oh, what am I going to do? I can't model in the show like this! I look *awful*!'

Twink and Kiki exchanged a worried glance. As Sooze had said, it was true that fairy hair grew quickly – Bimi would have her long locks back in just a month or so. But meanwhile, the exhibition was only a few days away.

'Well, I think you should model the dress anyway,' said Kiki staunchly. 'Your hair will look really cute by then – sort of short and spiky.'

Bimi sat up. 'I don't *want* short, spiky hair!' she wailed. 'I want my old hair back!' Bursting into loud sobs, she flung herself face down again, covering her head with her cotton-bud pillow.

Sooze looked stricken. 'Bimi, I'm really sorry,' she said in a small voice. 'It . . . it was just supposed to liven things up, that's all. I could try to get you a wig or something –'

'I don't want a wig! Just leave me alone!' sobbed Bimi.

Kiki hovered on her other side. 'Bimi, *please* say you'll still wear the dress,' she implored. 'You'll look beautiful, I promise.'

The rest of the branch echoed agreement. 'Look at Jax!' added Sili brightly. 'She wears her hair that way on *purpose.*'

But nothing anybody said made any difference, and Bimi lay crying until after the glow-worms were turned out. Twink, lying in her mossy bed beside her, felt her heart ache for Bimi. If only there was something she could do!

The day of the exhibition dawned bright and clear. Glitterwings Academy seemed to sparkle in the autumn sunshine. Each of its leaves had been polished, and long garlands of red and yellow flowers hung from its branches. A greeting spelled out in fairy dust – *Welcome Parents!* – hung shimmering over the tree.

The parents started arriving after lunch. Twink peeked out from behind the curtain of the changing area and saw crowds of them streaming into the Great Branch, sitting on the rows of mushroom seats that awaited them.

Excitement trembled through Twink as she spotted her own parents swooping in, looking proud and expectant. Oh, she could hardly wait for them to see the fashion show! They'd be so impressed at all the hard work everyone had put in.

Twink's eagerness faded as she caught sight of Bimi, sitting at a mushroom dressing table and staring glumly at herself. As Kiki had predicted, her hair had grown to a short, spiky length, framing her face like a blue explosion.

Making her way through the crowds of buzzing students, Twink perched on the edge of Bimi's dressing table. 'You look really pretty,' she offered.

It was true, she thought. Bimi would be beautiful no matter what she did with her hair. The short

style even suited her, making her blue eyes look
larger.

But Bimi clearly didn't agree. She pulled a face,
and didn't answer. 'I suppose you think this is what
I get for being *stuck-up*,' she said finally.

Twink gasped. 'Bimi, of course not! I'd never –'

'Oh, leave me alone!' said Bimi, looking close to
tears. 'Don't you have to go and put on your dress?'
She was already wearing hers, having reluctantly
agreed that she'd still model it . . . but it was clear
that all the joy had gone out of it for her.

Twink sighed and took the hint. Pushing through

a group of jabbering First Years, she found an empty space and put on her dandelion-leaf dress, adjusting the spiky cap on her head. She couldn't help smiling at herself in the mirror. Kiki had been right – the unusual dress was really something special!

A hush fell over the Branch. 'Ooh, this is it!' squealed Sili. Her silver hair shone like a waterfall over her bright blue top.

The fairies listened expectantly as Miss Shimmery greeted their parents. Then the lights dimmed, and the First Years flew out from the changing area to perform a dance they had devised themselves. Peering out through the curtain again, Twink saw them spinning and twirling in matching oak-leaf dresses.

Thunderous applause echoed through the Branch as the First Years returned, looking flushed and happy. 'It's us now!' whispered Kiki urgently. 'Get ready, everyone! Jax, quick, go and sort the glow-worms!'

'And now, from our Second Years . . . a fashion show!' came Miss Shimmery's voice.

The lights dimmed again. As the cricket band

started up its jazzy tune, Sooze and Lola swooped out through the curtains together. Twink heard a burst of applause as they flew down the aisle, posing and pouting like fashion stars. The audience began clapping along with the music, obviously enjoying the show hugely.

As the next pair of models flew out, Twink glanced at Bimi again – and her throat tightened. The blue-haired fairy's head was in her hands, her shoulders shaking. Kiki hovered worriedly beside her. 'Bimi, it'll be OK! You look great, you really do!'

'I just can't do it,' wept Bimi. 'I look like a hedgehog!'

Twink edged closer, her heart thudding. She had to do something! Suddenly, lying on a nearby table, she saw a sharpened stone that one of the upper years had used to trim a bit of ribbon.

Without thinking, Twink snatched it up. Pulling off her cap, she started grabbing up great handfuls of her long pink hair, hacking it off as short as she could.

'Twink, what are you *doing*?' cried Kiki, turning to stare at her. Bimi looked up too, and Twink heard her startled gasp.

Finished, Twink stared at her own reflection. Her hair stuck out in all directions, spiky and defiant. She popped the cap back on to her head and grinned at Bimi. 'Now we *both* look like hedgehogs,' she said firmly. 'We'll go on together!'

Bimi looked stunned. 'But – but Twink, you –'

'Come on, it's almost our turn!' Clasping Bimi's hand, Twink pulled her to the curtain.

As the two fairies waited to go on, Bimi whispered, 'Twink, you were right. I – I suppose I did get carried away with it all.'

Twink looked at her in surprise. Bimi's cheeks were on fire. 'I just . . . never enjoyed being pretty before. It sort of went to my head. But you're right; I've been acting really stupid – preening over myself like a total wasp brain! I'm sorry I got so cross with you for pointing it out.'

'Oh, but *I'm* sorry for how I acted all term!' cried Twink. 'I was *awful*. I don't blame you for getting fed up with me.'

'But that crystal prophecy – you must have been so upset!' shivered Bimi. 'I'd have acted just the same way.' She hesitated, biting her lip. 'Twink . . . do you think we could be best friends again? I've really missed you!'

'Oh, yes!' cried Twink.

The two fairies hugged tightly, fluttering their wings. A warm glow spread through Twink like sunshine. At last, she had her best friend back!

'Do this later, you two!' laughed Kiki, shoving

them from behind their wings. 'You're on!'

Linking arms, Twink and Bimi exchanged a grin and flew out from behind the curtain. Jax's spotlight hit them firmly as they stopped to hover, showing off their dresses – Twink's with spikes, Bimi's with stars, and both models with matching hair!

The two friends smiled at each other as the audience cheered.

'Now!' whispered Bimi, her eyes gleaming. And as though they had practised it for weeks, they pirouetted down the flyway together, their wings flashing.

Twink's heart felt light as a feather as she spun and twirled. She knew her parents were somewhere out there in the darkness, proud of her. And perhaps the Second Year would win the prize for best exhibition, or perhaps not . . . but Twink knew that she had already won the best prize of all!

Turn over the page
and read the glimmery
beginning of Twink's
next adventure

From Seedling Exams

Chapter One

Twink Flutterby's heart quickened as she and her parents crested the icy hill. Any moment now . . . any moment . . . and then all at once, there it was! Glitterwings Academy, its bare branches sparkling with frost in the winter sunshine.

Hurrah, good old Glitterwings! thought Twink. Even if this term wasn't going to be the easiest, she was still pleased to be back.

'Oh, isn't it lovely this time of year!' breathed Twink's mother. Twink's father chuckled, and he and Twink exchanged an amused glance. Twink's mother *always* thought her old school looked wonderful, no matter what the season.

But she was right, thought Twink as they swooped to land on the frozen front lawn, where crowds of returning students were milling about with their parents. Her school *was* the most beautiful in the world!

Glitterwings Academy was located inside a massive oak tree on a hill. Tiny golden windows wound their way up its trunk, and a set of grand double doors sat at its base. Glancing upwards, Twink picked out Peony Branch, where she and her friends had lived for the past three terms. Excitement darted through her. She could hardly wait to see everyone again!

Miss Shimmery, the HeadFairy, flew forward to greet them, her rainbow wings gleaming like icicles. 'Twink, welcome back! Are you ready for the Seedling Exams?'

Twink's stomach tightened abruptly at the thought of the important exams waiting for her at the end of the term. 'I – I think so,' she said,

trying to smile.

'I'm sure you'll do well.' Miss Shimmery's blue eyes were kind. 'It's Creature Kindness you're especially interested in, isn't it?'

'That's right,' put in Twink's father proudly. 'She wants to be a Fairy Medic, just like her parents.'

An embarrassed flush lit Twink's cheeks. 'Dad!' she hissed. It was true that being a Fairy Medic was all she'd ever wanted to do, but he didn't have to *tell* everyone!

Miss Shimmery laughed. 'Well, I'm sure you'll make a splendid medic. Have a good term, Twink – and don't worry, you'll do fine.' She flitted off in a flash of snowy-white hair.

Miss Sparkle, the dour second-year head, was standing on one of the tree's frosted roots, checking in her students. Once Twink had been ticked off the list, her father handed her her oak-leaf bag.

'Don't worry about the exams. Just do your best, Twinkster,' he said, gently ruffling her long pink hair. 'That's all we want.'

'We'll be proud of you no matter how you do,

darling,' her mother assured her with a hug. 'We know you'll try hard.'

Twink waved as her parents flew off, watching until they disappeared over the hill. Then she dropped her arm with a sigh. Her mum and dad might *say* they didn't mind if she didn't do well in her exams . . . but deep down, Twink knew they'd be disappointed. They were so pleased that she wanted to follow in their wing strokes!

'Twink!' cried a voice.

Twink spun about and saw Bimi Bluebell, her best friend, flying rapidly towards her. The two fairies met with an excited hug, wings fluttering. 'I'm so glad to see you!' said Twink.

'Me too,' said Bimi, pushing back a strand of dark blue hair. 'Oh, but Twink, I'm so nervous! I can't believe we have the Seedlings this term!'